250
Old growth

1000

ure forest

ANCIENT ONES

ANCIENT ONES

The World of the Old-Growth Douglas Fir

BARBARA BASH

TREE
TALES

Sierra Club Books for Children
San Francisco

The Sierra Club, founded in 1892 by John Muir, has devoted itself to the study and protection of the earth's scenic and ecological resources — mountains, wetlands, woodlands, wild shores and rivers, deserts and plains. The publishing program of the Sierra Club offers books to the public as a nonprofit educational service in the hope that they may enlarge the public's understanding of the Club's basic concerns. The Sierra Club has some sixty chapters in the United States and in Canada. For information about how you may participate in its programs to preserve wilderness and the quality of life, please address inquiries to Sierra Club, 730 Polk Street, San Francisco, CA 94109.

First Edition

All calligraphy by Barbara Bash

Acknowledgments
The author wishes to thank Chris Maser for his enormous help with the research and the manuscript, and Helen Sweetland for her endless patience and support throughout the making of this book. Thanks also to Joe Spieler for his good eye and ear, Andy Moldenke and Jim Werntz at Oregon State University for their help with the bugs, and Jim Sedell for his kind introduction to the old-growth world.

Library of Congress Cataloging-in-Publication Data
Bash, Barbara.
    Ancient ones : the world of the old-growth Douglas fir / Barbara Bash. — 1st ed.
        p.   cm. — (Tree tales)
    ISBN 0-87156-561-7 (acid-free paper)
    1. Douglas fir — Northwest, Pacific — Juvenile literature. 2. Douglas fir — Northwest, Pacific — Life cycles — Juvenile literature. 3. Forest ecology — Northwest, Pacific — Juvenile literature. [1. Douglas fir. 2. Old growth forests. 3. Forest ecology.
4. Ecology.] I. Title II. Series: Bash, Barbara. Tree tales.
QK494.5.P66B35   1994
585'.2 — dc20   93-45251

10 9 8 7 6 5 4 3 2 1

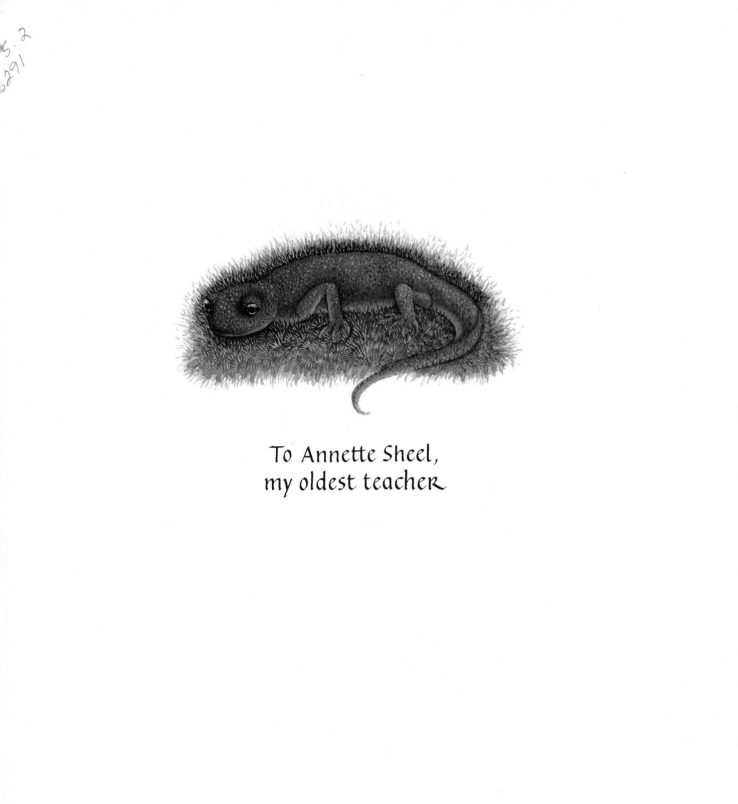

To Annette Sheel,
my oldest teacher

Walking into an old-growth forest, you enter a strangely silent world. The earth feels moist and springy underfoot, and the air is thick with the fragrance of decomposing needles. Lichen-covered logs crisscross the forest floor, and moss clings to the towering trunks. At first, it all seems too quiet and still. But after a while, you start to relax — and begin to really look and listen.

High overhead, in the canopy of branches, a bird warbles softly. Out of the corner of your eye, you see a seed (or is it a pine needle?) drift lazily to the cushioned floor. This is the world of the Ancient Ones — silent, enormous, and full of secrets.

The old-growth forests of the Pacific Northwest extend along the coast from northern California to southeastern Alaska. Many different trees inhabit this world. Amid lacy layers of hemlock and vine maple, mixed stands of spruce and cedar stretch to the sky. But the mighty Douglas fir towers over everything. Reaching heights of more than three hundred feet— taller than a twenty-story building—it is one of the largest living things on earth. Many Douglas firs live for five hundred years; some make it to a thousand. Over the centuries, these giants show their age much as people do, becoming furrowed, craggy, and full of character.

You crane your neck way back to see the treetops. Who is living up in those branches?

Many animals make their homes in the soft moss and lichen that collect on the wide branches of the canopy. After a day of catching fish in the Pacific Ocean, marbled murrelets fly more than thirty miles to nest on these soft platforms. Among the branches, tiny rufous hummingbirds construct cups out of moss, needles, and spiderwebs to hold their eggs. Douglas squirrels, in search of ripe fir cones, also visit these lush aerial gardens perched more than one hundred fifty feet above the ground.

Red tree voles may spend their entire lives up here, never touching the forest floor. When they are hungry, they eat Douglas fir needles; when they are thirsty, they lick the dew off wet branches.

In the old-growth world, dead trees, called snags, are truly the life of the forest, because they house many more creatures than live trees do. Pileated woodpeckers hollow out cavities, which are later taken over by families of bluebirds. Vaux swifts construct nests inside hollow snags, attaching twigs to the walls with their gluey saliva. An osprey builds a big stick nest on the very top of a dying tree.

At twilight, these birds settle into their hollows and other creatures begin to stir. A flying squirrel peeks out of its den. A big brown bat, hidden under a loosening piece of bark, stretches out its soft, leathery wings. Soon these night creatures will be darting and gliding among the darkening trees.

Deep in the night, a flying squirrel parachutes down to the forest floor to dig for truffles, the fruit of a special fungus. A female spotted owl also leaves her nest at the top of a broken-off tree. She is in search of food, too, and follows the squirrel down with silent wings and sharp talons. If she catches it, she will be able to take a meal home to the owlets waiting in her nest.

Longhorn beetle

Enlarged 2 times

Golden buprestid

Enlarged 3 times

Bark beetle

Enlarged 5 times

On the forest floor, newly fallen snags become pathways for long-tailed weasels and tiny mice. Bark beetles chew under the bark, engraving delicate galleries where they deposit their eggs.

Soon longhorn beetles and golden buprestids move in, digging deeper tunnels and opening the log for more creatures to enter. As the beetles burrow, they leave behind fungal spores (the seeds of a fungus), which they've carried in on their bodies. The fungus begins to branch out in fine threads that penetrate the wood. The slow recycling of the dead tree is under way.

Sometimes snags fall across streams, slowing the current and creating quiet pools. The fallen logs sift and clean the water by trapping debris long enough for it to be broken down by aquatic insects. The insects, in turn, become food for coho salmon, which swim upstream from the ocean to spawn. Tailed frogs and Olympic salamanders forage in the gentle riffles, while dragonflies and long-tailed mayflies dart over the water's surface. A Pacific giant salamander, the largest land salamander in the world, lays her eggs where the water can flow steadily over them. She will guard them for almost nine months until they hatch.

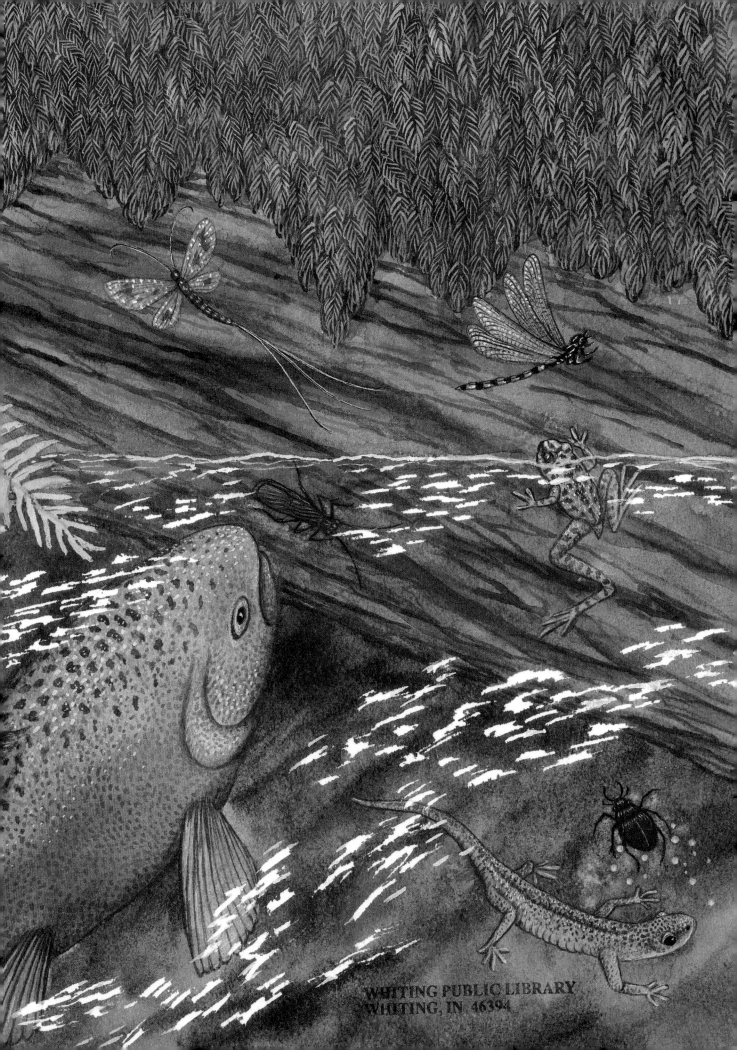

Termites

Termites

Enlarged 2 times

The more a log decays, the more it splits and crumbles. Wide cracks extend along its length, creating openings like secret cave dwellings. Out of these dark caverns sprout colorful mushrooms, the fruit of the spreading fungi deep inside the log. Snail-eating beetles move quickly over the rough wood. A huge banana slug slides slowly under a honey mushroom, nibbling on the delicate gills. A Pacific tree frog hides in the moss atop the log, while a tiny shrew-mole burrows into the soft wood below. Deep inside, thousands of termites dig a vast network of tiny passages.

Millipedes and sow bugs probe
their way through the tunnels dug
by the termites. They chew up the
log, leaving behind droppings that
look like jigsaw puzzles made up
of tiny wood chips. Fungi feed
on the wood, too, their slender
threads reaching everywhere. In
dark crevices, pseudoscorpions
build silken nests and wait for
unsuspecting beetles to wander past.

Sow bug

Pseudoscorpion

Millipede

Fungal threads

Enlarged 12 times

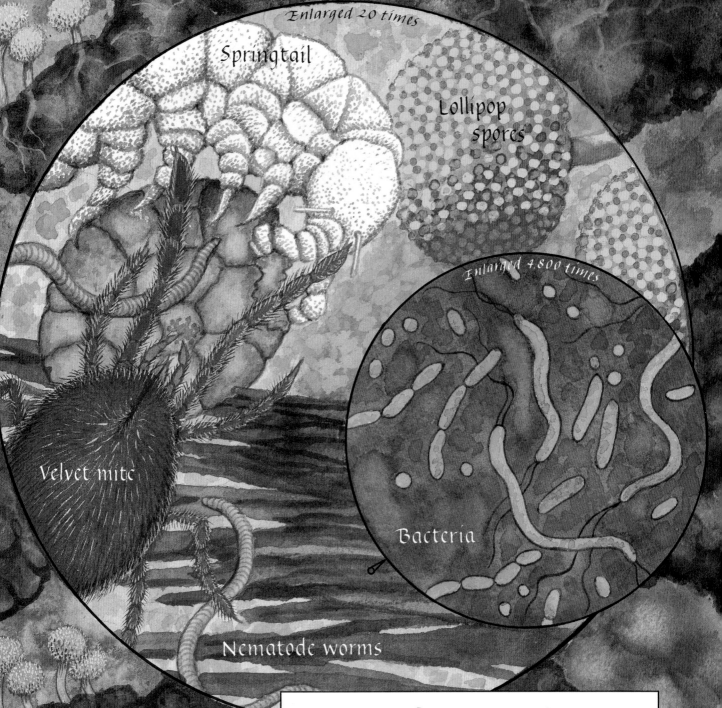

Springtail

Lollipop
spores

Enlarged 4,800 times

Velvet mite

Bacteria

Nematode worms

Hundreds of thousands of even
smaller creatures also move
through the deep passages. Tiny
mites and springtails devour the
pellets left by the millipedes and
sow bugs. Finally, billions of
microscopic bacteria break the
wood down into finer and finer bits.

After five hundred years, a fallen snag is nothing more than a soft mound of earth. All the grinding and tunneling have turned the wood into powdery, rich soil. Hemlock saplings and huckleberries sprout from this ground, providing food for Roosevelt elk in winter. But a Douglas fir cannot grow in this sheltered world. In order for _it_ to sprout, a dramatic event must occur—one that happens only once every two hundred fifty to four hundred years.

It usually happens in summer, when a thunderstorm builds overhead. Suddenly lightning strikes a towering Douglas fir, and a hot bead of fire travels down the trunk, igniting the dry underbrush. With winds fanning the flames, the wildfire rages quickly through the forest. Some trees survive the intense heat; others do not. But the death of these trees brings new life to the forest, because it allows sunlight to reach the soil again — and a Douglas fir must have sunlight in order to sprout.

A few months after the fire,
cooling rains begin. The
winged seeds of the surviving
Douglas firs break loose from
their cones and spin down to
the ground. As deer mice and
Townsend chipmunks explore the
charred forest, looking for seeds
to eat, they leave behind droppings
full of the live spores of their
favorite food, the truffle. With
these droppings, the mice and
chipmunks unknowingly help
prepare the soil for new trees.

A Douglas fir seed lands next to a fallen tree and escapes the notice of the busy animals. The following spring, it swells and splits open in the warm, rich soil. The seedling's tiny roots reach out and burrow into a mouse dropping, finding thousands of truffle spores. The fungus that grows from these spores forms a coating around the root tips, protecting them from disease and bringing to the seedling nutrients from the soil. At the same time, the seedling begins to send sugar to the fungus, making it grow faster. Every Douglas fir seedling, if it is to survive, must form a partnership with this special fungus.

In the sunlit clearing, surrounded
and protected by its elders, the tiny
Douglas fir becomes a sapling. Over
the centuries, it will grow straight
and tall, then scarred and deeply
furrowed. Finally, weakened by
insects and toppled by wind or fire,
it will sink slowly back into the soil
to nourish the future.

Author's Note

I made two trips to the old-growth forests of the Pacific Northwest in the course of creating this book. At first, I was overwhelmed by the dense layers of growth in these woods. I kept looking for some order — a nice, neat stand of old growth. But the more time I spent in the forest, the more the "disorder" made sense. Everything was happening at once — growing, dying, falling over, sprouting up — and somehow I had to capture it all.

I spent many hours in those tangled woods, watching and listening. I climbed over fallen logs, crouched by rushing streams, napped in sunlit clearings, and hiked in the rain. Sitting and sketching under the enormous trees, I began to relax. Somehow the book would get done. I felt there was enough time to learn about this old-growth world — and to find my place in it.

But there may not be much time left for the ancient trees themselves. One hundred fifty years ago, the old-growth forests stretched over millions of acres of the Northwest. Today less than ten percent of these forests remain — a patchwork of small woods surrounded by clearcuts. In some areas, lumber companies have replanted. But tree farms are a far cry from the diverse and complex worlds that once stood in their place. We've learned a sad lesson: Though we can plant trees, we cannot plant a forest. Unless we work to preserve and protect them, the last of the Ancient Ones — and the intricate web of life they support — will disappear forever from the Earth.

1 YEAR
Grasses
& herbs

15
Shrubs
& seedlings

30
Shrubs
& saplings

50
young forest